3 4028 09363 2355
HARRIS COUNTY PUBLIC LIBRARY

JPIC
Stea
W9-AJR-188
The only fish in the sea

$17.99
ocn953842575
First edition.

WITHDRAWN

huff huff huff huff

"Hey, Sadie! Did you hear about Little Amy Scott?
About how she got a goldfish for her birthday, and then said out loud . . .

GOLDFISH ARE BORING!

"And how she walked all the way out of town, past the empty school bus,
and down to the dock where Jacob Finney's been asleep for as long as I can remember?"

"Imagine that poor fish all alone, floating away, and away, and away. He must feel like . . .

To Lily Anna —P. S.

To Phil —M. C.

Text copyright © 2017 by Philip C. Stead
Illustrations copyright © 2017 by Matthew Cordell
A Neal Porter Book
Published by Roaring Brook Press
Roaring Brook Press is a division of Holtzbrinck Publishing Holdings Limited Partnership
175 Fifth Avenue, New York, New York 10010
The artwork for this book was created using pen and ink with watercolor.
mackids.com
All rights reserved

Cataloging-in-Publication Data is on file at the Library of Congress

ISBN: 978-1-62672-282-8

Our books may be purchased in bulk for promotional, educational, or business use. Please contact your local bookseller or the Macmillan Corporate and Premium Sales Department at (800) 221-7945 ext. 5442 or by e-mail at MacmillanSpecialMarkets@macmillan.com.

First edition 2017
Book design by Philip C. Stead and Matthew Cordell
Printed in China by RR Donnelley Asia printing Solutions Ltd.,Dongguan City,Guangdong Province

1 3 5 7 9 10 8 6 4 2

written by
Philip C. Stead

illustrated by
Matthew Cordell

A Neal Porter Book
Roaring Brook Press
New York

"What do you think about that, Sadie? . . . Sadie?"

"That's terrible, Sherman."

"Because the sea is awfully big . . .

. . . and there are a lot of dangers to face."

SCOPE & OPTICAL
MAPS
Sundries
bric-a-brac
click!

"The important thing, Sherman, is that Ellsworth stays hopeful and brave, knowing that we're on our way."

"Hey, Sadie, wait! Who's Ellsworth?"

"Sherman, you have to keep up. Every fish deserves a proper name."

BOAT
COME ON IN

"Now, we'll need to borrow a boat . . .

a net, and two long fishing poles . . .

twenty-one pink balloons . . .

a bucket of paint . . .

and appropriate headwear in case of weather—good or bad.

Then, with any luck, Sherman . . .

we'll catch a fish in time for dinner."

WELCOME HOME ELLSWORTH
POP!

"In the meantime, we'll have tea. Patience, Sherman, is the most important part of fishing."

KAW!

WE CO O E LLSWORTH
POP
slurrrpppp...
sip... sip...

WOOLWORTH

"Sadie?"

"Yes, Sherman?"

"Are we eating Ellsworth
for dinner tonight?"

"Sherman, no!"

"We'll give him a home and find him a nice place to sit and be a fish—

POST
OFFICE
MUSEUM

somewhere with a view
of the entire neighborhood."

"When he is hungry we will feed him."

"And when he is lonely
we will keep him company."

"Ellsworth will feel lucky to have so many friends."

FOOD
FOR
FISHES
PBBT!
click!

"Sadie?"

"Yes, Sherman?"

"What about Little Amy Scott?"

"Sherman, she'll spend her birthday alone."

"And that's all right."

Harris County Public Library
Houston, Texas